AF379662

SIGNERELLA

Signerella

Starr Lewis

Charleston, SC
www.PalmettoPublishing.com

Signerella
Copyright © 2020 by Starr Lewis

All rights reserved
No portion of this book may be reproduced, stored in a retrieval system, or transmitted
in any form by any means–electronic, mechanical, photocopy, recording, or other–except
for brief quotations in printed reviews, without prior permission of the author.

ISBN-13: 978-1-64990-283-2
ISBN-10: 1-64990-283-2

ACKNOWLEDGMENTS

Special thanks to Dr. John Reid, Daniela Alvarez, and all those who helped me along the way - you know who you are.

A NOTE ON THE TEXT

In *Signerella,* many characters communicate through American Sign Language. While this is similar to spoken English, it is an entirely different language and will be written in its own unique way. As the author, I would like to make it completely clear that my use of written Sign Language in this story is in no way meant to be disrespectful, and it should not be misread as any sort of slight against the language. I have written in this manner to be faithful to the way that members of the deaf community would actually communicate, and have done so with the utmost respect and admiration for Sign Language and the deaf community as a whole. Thank you.

Prologue

In the country of Spain long ago, a beautiful baby girl was born to Annalise and John Jimenez. Her name was Isabella, and she lived a happy and peaceful life with her mother and father. Isabella, however, was unique. She was born deaf, and her parents began to teach her sign language at a very young age. They raised Isabella to believe that her deafness was not a disability or a birth defect, as others would say, but that it was just another part of her that made her special. Despite the judgmental and often cruel behavior of others, Isabella always felt safe and loved by her mother and father.

Things were good in the Jimenez home for a time, until Annalise fell ill and died when Isabella was 12 years old. John and Isabella struggled to deal with the loss of Annalise, but did their absolute best to support each other. Within a year, however, John met a new woman, a widow named Margret. They courted for a short time, and married by the time Isabella was 14. Isabella's new stepmother had two children of her own, 16 year old Elsbeth and 19 year old Reginald. Isabella's new step siblings were quite spoiled, and were jealous of the attention she got from John. When John was away, Reginald and Elsbeth would make fun of Isabella when she tried to use sign language to communicate with them. Still, things settled into a new routine, and Isabella was peaceful with her father and step family. Four years passed, and then tragedy struck. While on trip to a nearby kingdom, John died. From then on, Margret began to treat Isabella as a servant, slaving away in the house each and every day. Without her parents, Isabella struggled, spending each day alone in her tiny attic room when she wasn't working for or being mocked by her step family. She felt that nobody understood her or really cared about her. Still, Isabella tried her best to have hope and believe that someday, she would show the world what she was really capable of.

Scene One

Early on a summer morning, the sun was just beginning to rise over the trees. Dew glistened on the leaves and the plants as the small village of Liata started to wake up. The smells of baking bread wafted through the open windows on a cool breeze, and there was a peaceful feeling in the air. In a small, dark red cottage on the edge of town, Isabella leaned out the window of her attic bedroom, watching the sunrise. She smiled as a Golden Eagle perched on a nearby branch, then signed to it in greeting.

ISABELLA
Hello beautiful bird! I want free just like eagle flying. One day I will. I believe I will. Now, I not.

Isabella watched thoughtfully as the bird flew up to a higher branch. When it landed, the eagle turned its head, almost as if looking directly at her.

ISABELLA

Eagle fly away, amazing! I wish same, fly away. Wish have wings same. Room here, me out fly, eagle join. Every morning eagle I watch, come up with name. Name you G-i-l-b-e-r-t-o. Brief B-e-t-o.

Beto ruffled his feathers, and Isabella gave a sad smile.

ISABELLA

You eagle beautiful, you don't know you really beautiful. You special eagle, fly around, none judge you. Me, people think young, deaf, clueless. Hearing people judge me useless.

Isabella continued to lean out the window, watching and signing to Beto as he flew away.

ISABELLA

Bye, see you tomorrow morning, free fly.

While Isabella leaned out the window, taking in the beautiful morning, Elsbeth came marching into the small room, slamming the door open. She looked around the room with distaste and saw Isabella in the window. Elsbeth folded her arms and shook her head, then smirked meanly and walked up to Isabella. Isabella didn't notice Elsbeth approaching until she was standing right behind her. Elsbeth tapped her hard on the shoulder, and Isabella turned to look at her with dread.

ELSBETH

And just what is going on in here?

She started to mock Isabella, waving her arms and hands around and pretending to use sign language. Isabella was hurt, but just shook her head and started reading Elsbeth's lips as she spoke.

ELSBETH

Sooo sorry to interrupt your morning, *your highness*. But you are late, so stop dragging your feet. It's time for you to get downstairs, prepare Mother's clothes and mine, and get our breakfast ready. Honestly, we shouldn't have to tell you this all the time.

Isabella just looked at Elsbeth for a moment, having a hard time keeping up and reading her words as fast as Elsbeth was speaking. Elsbeth huffed and rolled her eyes.

ELSBETH

Ugh, do you understand anything? Get... down... stairs... and... get... to... work... STUPID!

With that, she gave Isabella one last nasty look, then turned on her heel and walked out of the room. Isabella stood alone in the room. She sighed deeply, then turned and took one last look out the window before walking out.

ISABELLA (thinking)

One day, they will know I am human, just like them.

Scene Two

Meanwhile, across the kingdom in the *Castillo del Escorial*, the royal family sat together for breakfast. Prince Misael, the only son of the king and queen, stood sullenly looking out of the small window of the private dining area where he had breakfast with his parents, King Philippe and Queen Marisol. Eating breakfast at the table behind him, the king and queen exchanged worried looks.

PHILIPPE

Why don't you come eat some breakfast, son? You haven't been eating enough recently. We've had all of your favorite foods prepared!

MISAEL

Thank you, really. But please, don't try to ply me with food. I'm fine, just... thinking. I have a lot on my mind.

Misael turned back to the window. King Philippe looked at Queen Marisol and gave a small shrug. She widened her eyes at him and nodded her head toward Misael.

MARISOL (mouths)
Do something!

King Philippe huffed, then cleared his throat and spoke to the queen loudly so that Misael could hear him.

PHILIPPE
Well darling, I've been thinking. It's high time we had a ball for the kingdom. *Si, si,* a grand ball. Don't you think that sounds like a good idea *mi amor?*

Queen Marisol raised her eyebrows and smiled with understanding. She responded, also speaking up loudly.

MARISOL
Si! A ball sounds like a wonderful idea. We can invite people from all around the kingdom, and we shall have plenty of food, drink, music, and dancing. A ball will put everyone in high spirits I think.

PHILIPPE
Indeed! It will be *maravilloso*! What do you think son? A ball would be great fun for all of us.

Misael shook his head and turned to his parents with a small, exasperated smile. He walked around the table to speak with his parents.

MISAEL
Mama, Papa. I love you both dearly. You are wonderful, and I know that you would both do anything to make me happy. I do so enjoy it when the castle is open for such festivity.

The king and queen smiled and nodded encouragingly.

MISAEL

However, this time I feel differently. I think I have grown tired
of all the same things, all of the same faces at every ball, seeing
me only as the prince. I wish they could see that I am not just
some prince.

The prince sat at the table sadly. Philippe and Marisol exchanged
a troubled look.

PHILIPPE

Son, I am sure I do not understand. You want people NOT to
think of you as royalty? You come from royal blood! *Mira*.

The king pointed at the far wall, where royal portraits of past
kings were displayed. Misael looked thoughtfully at the portraits,
then back at his father.

PHILIPPE

These are your ancestors, Misael. This kingdom has been
carried by the Escorial bloodline for the last seven generations.
You are an Escorial, and someday this will all be yours. Surely
you cannot mean that you dislike being royalty?

Misael shook his head emphatically.

MISAEL

No, that is not it. It is a privilege to be a part of this family, and
I intend to rule with the same justice and wisdom that you have

always shown. What I mean to say is that I wonder who I will have to share all of this with? I have yet to meet anyone who really understands me, or who I could see myself spending the rest of my life with. I mean, most of the kingdom is not even aware that I am hard of hearing! That is a big part of who I am, and if I cannot share such an important part of myself, how can I share the rest of my life?

MARISOL

Oh Misa, I did not realize that this has been troubling you so. Your hearing changes nothing.

PHILIPPE

Your mother is right. You may be hard of hearing, but we made sure that you had the best tutors. You can read lips and speak fluently in English and *Espanol*. And let us not forget that you are able to speak with your hands, which is a special skill that very few in this kingdom have.

MARISOL

You should be proud of your abilities!

MISAEL

I know, and I am. I suppose I am not explaining myself well enough. Never mind, I am sorry. I will get over these feelings eventually.

MARISOL

No Misa, we just want to help you. Please explain. We will not try to fix it for you, we will just listen.

Marisol searched Misael's face earnestly. He met her gaze for a moment, then looked back down at the table. Misael spoke without making eye contact with either of his parents.

MISAEL

I want nothing more than to share this kingdom with a love of my own. I am lonely, and I just want someone who belongs with me. Someone... different.

Marisol reached across the table to take Misael's hand. He looked up at her, and she nodded encouragingly. Philippe leaned forward to get his son's attention and spoke.

PHILIPPE

Go on son. I understand not wanting to be alone, but what do you mean when you say "different"?

MISAEL

I mean someone who really cares about me as a person, about who I truly am. I am proud to be descended from a long line of God-fearing, strong leaders. But I want someone who will look deeper and see that I have more to offer - that I am only human too.

Misael finished speaking and looked hesitantly at his parents to see how they would react.

MISAEL

Does that make sense, or do you both think I'm crazy for this?

Marisol and Philippe passed an understanding look between them and turned back to Misael.

PHILIPPE

Si, claro. We understand you perfectly well son. You are at an age where you start to consider your future seriously, and realizing that you do not want to spend it alone. As a matter of fact, I was around your age when I fell in love with your mother. But remember son, you are only 22 years old. Be patient, and you will find the right person in time... just as I did with *mi amor.*

Marisol smiled lovingly at Philippe, then addressed her son.

MARISOL

Exactly. Any love worth having takes time; you just have to wait for it. In the meantime, you have family and friends, and an entire kingdom that loves you. We should still celebrate all that we have been blessed with.

Misael nodded and gave a short laugh.

MISAEL

I know what that means... we are having a ball. I suppose it could be fun.

PHILIPPE

Marvilloso! We will have this grand ball then. It will be good for you son, and for us all. When shall it be?

MARISOL

Wonderful, I am so excited! Well, we will need time to send out the word and prepare the feast. We shall hold the ball in one week!

PHILIPPE

Very well then, a ball it is!

MISAEL

A ball it is.

MARISOL

Goodness, I have so much to do. One week until the ball!

Marisol snapped and called for a maid, who appeared quickly.

MARISOL

Ana, fetch me the scribe. We need to spread the word... we are having a ball!

Ana curtsied and left the room, and the family all smiled at one another in excitement and anticipation.

Scene Three

Early the next morning, the royal messengers went far and wide throughout the kingdom, spreading the word about the ball. In Liata, the people buzzed with excitement as they read the announcements posted throughout the town square.

TOWN MEMBER #1

My goodness, a ball? This is so exciting! I have so much to do if I am going to charm the prince: my hair, my clothes...

TOWN MEMBER #2

I'm so excited that the ball is open to the whole kingdom. Think of all the different people we shall meet!

TOWN MEMBER #3

Ha! I tell you what, if I had what the king and queen have, I certainly wouldn't be throwing any balls. I would keep all that lovely money for myself!

As the people milled about the town square talking and shopping at different vendors, Isabella arrived to do the household shopping as her stepmother ordered her to do. As she looked around, Isabella was reminded of all the times that she had gone to the market as a child with her mother, and the fun that they had. She gave a small, sad smile and shook herself out of the memory. Isabella walked up to Henriquez, the only vendor who would communicate with her in Sign Language. Henriquez had been friends with Isabella's father, and was one of the few people in town who showed her true kindness. Isabella walked up to him with a smile, and he smiled back warmly before signing to her. Henriuez's sign language was sparse, so he spoke as he signed so she could read any words that he did not know how to sign.

HENRIQUEZ

Good morning I-s-a-b-e-l-l-a!

ISABELLA

Good morning! See, what I want...

HENRIQUEZ

Fresh! Fruit, nuts, sweets we have. Take much you want.

Isabella nodded as Henriquez signed, then looked down at her stepmother's list. She signed to Henriquez as she looked around the tables.

ISABELLA

Yes, nice, shiny, new! Ten apples, one vine, nuts I buy.

HENRIQUEZ
Perfect!

While Henriquez went to prepare her groceries, Isabella looked around the market, curiously noticing all the people walking and talking with even more excitement than usual. Henriquez came back over with her packages, and Isabella paid him, then packed her fruit in the basket she brought with her. She signed to Henriquez.

ISABELLA
Today store open later? Want to buy fish, rice.

HENRIQUEZ
Sorry, not night. My wife, me-

As Henriquez was in the middle of signing to Isabella, a woman came bustling up and interrupted, standing right in front of Isabella as if she was not there and speaking to Henriquez.

WOMAN
Buenos dias Henriquez! Have you heard the news? A royal ball in just one week... and the whole kingdom is invited! Will you and your *señora* be there?

Isabella stepped to the side slightly and tried to read the woman's lips as she spoke excitedly, but could only catch a few words. Henriquez glanced over at her before addressing the woman.

HENRIQUEZ

Well yes, we did hear about the ball. It is all anyone can talk
about this morning! I am sure my wife would never let me hear
the end of it if we did not go. But if you will excuse me Señora
Melendez, I was speaking with a customer when you arrived.

He gestured to Isabella, who gave a small smile and nod as the
woman looked her up and down uncomfortably. Señora Melendez
gave an insincere half smile, then turned on her heel and stalked
off. Henriquez gave Isabella an apologetic shrug as she began to
sign to him again.

ISABELLA

What's up? I miss something... they excited, what for?

HENRIQUEZ

Saturday next, big fancy party. B-a-l-l happening with royal
family! See announcement, here.

Henriquez looked around behind him and found a copy of
the royal announcement. He handed it to Isabella, who read
with growing interest. When she finished, Isabella looked
back up at Henriquez with a mixture of surprise and excitement. He smiled and nodded in understanding, then signed
to Isabella.

HENRIQUEZ

Yes, exciting! Tell family about party if they not know. Prince
want to meet you, beautiful.

Henriquez winked and smiled kindly. Isabella laughed and thanked him, then left. She walked home slowly, daydreaming and thinking about the royal ball.

Scene Four

Back at home, Elsbeth and Reginald practiced the waltz as a part of their daily dance lessons. Margret played the piano, barking commands at her children as they went through the steps.

MARGRET

Alright, now it's 1 2 3, 1 2 3, 1 2 3. Nice and graceful, 1 2 3... Come now Elsbeth! Dance with the rhythm - not ahead of it, not behind it, but *with* the rhythm.

Elsbeth got flustered and struggled to keep up with Reginald, tripping through the step and nearly falling to the ground. Reginald caught her, and as they straightened, he turned to Margret, exasperated.

REGINALD

It's no use Mother... this girl just has no rhythm. She's hopeless! And she's been bruising my poor feet for the last half hour.

ELSBETH

Well it's not my fault! *Your* feet were going the wrong direction,
you big dolt!

REGINALD

They were not! I was perfect as always, but you kept tripping
me up.

ELSBETH

Perfect? HA! You were not!

REGINALD

Oh yes I-

MARGRET

That is quite enough you two! Stop fussing and keep
practicing... you both need a lot of work. Elsbeth, you must
count the steps as you dance. Now, 1 2-

Before Elsbeth and Reginald could begin waltzing, the front
door burst open, and Isabella came in with the baskets from the
market. Margret glared as she entered, then stood and walked up
to her. Even though she knew some Sign Language from being
married to Isabella's father, Margret refused to sign to Isabella,
instead requiring her to read her lips as she spoke.

MARGRET

Isabella, it is about time you got back here. What took you so
long? Well anyway, don't just stand there - hurry up and get
those things put away so you can get started on our dinner.

Reginald and Elsbeth have worked up quite an appetite, so make it fast.

Isabella nodded, then turned to walk away. As she started to leave, Margret noticed the paper Isabella still clutched in her hand. Margret grabbed Isabella by the arm, stopping her, and snatched the paper.

MARGRET
Wait. And just what is this?

As she read the royal announcement, Margret gasped and turned to her children with a smile on her face. Reginald and Elsbeth watched her read with eager anticipation. They walked over to her, and Margret held the paper out to them wordlessly. Reginald took it from her hand and began to read while Elsbeth leaned over his shoulder, reading as well.

ELSBETH
Oh my goodness, a royal ball? This is my dream come true!

MARGRET
Yes my dear, a ball at the Castillo del Escorial!

Margret and Elsbeth hugged in excitement, and even Reginald looked pleased with the news. To the side of the room, Isabella sat down the basket she had been carrying and watched the family's reactions.

REGINALD

Well, even I'm excited! This is my chance to charm beautiful women from all over the kingdom. Not only that, I will meet Prince Misael in person. You know, if he and I are near the same age, perhaps we will become friends. With his riches and my charm and good looks, we would make a great team.

Reginald smirked arrogantly, then leaned towards his sister tauntingly.

REGINALD

And let me guess, Beth. You will want the prince to fall madly in love with you and sweep you off your feet to be his princess. I hate to break it to you, but as poorly as you dance, you'll have a better chance of the prince running away from you to protect his own feet.

Reginald laughed at his own joke, but Margret waved him away dismissively.

MARGRET

Oh stop it Reginald. My, we have so much to do! Elsbeth my dear, you will be at your most beautiful and charming of course, and the prince will certainly fall in love with you. And for added security, Reginald, when you befriend Prince Misael, do put in a word in your sister's favor.

Margret paced excitedly. Reginald rolled his eyes at his sister, but agreed to Margret's plan.

ELSBETH

What shall we wear? Perhaps we should all wear the same color, or at least coordinate so that we do not clash.

REGINALD

Oh come on, we can't match! Mother, I am an adult and I refuse to dress like my little sister.

ELSBETH

I don't know why you have a problem… I happen to have an excellent sense of style, unlike you.

Elsbeth flipped her hair over her shoulder in Reginald's face, and he rolled his eyes at her again.

MARGRET

Enough! This is no time for your petty quarreling. We have much to do before next Saturday.

From her spot in the corner, Isabella stepped forward hesitantly and waved her hands to get her stepmother's attention.

ELSBETH

Oh look, Isabella wants to "say" something.

REGINALD

You know she can't really "say" anything. What does she want Mother?

Margret narrowed her eyes and looked over at Isabella. She nodded once, and Isabella approached cautiously.

MARGRET

What is it now Isabella? What could you possibly want?

Isabella signed to Margret, but hesitated as Elsbeth and Reginald mocked her behind their mother's back, waving their hands around and pretending to sign. Margret snapped in Isabella's face and spoke sharply.

MARGRET

Focus! What do you want, girl?

Isabella began to sign again, going slowly so that Margret could follow along.

ISABELLA

B-a-l-l. I join can? Dancing.

Isabella acted as though she was dancing, in her head imagining herself at the ball. She curtsied, then moved into a perfect waltz. Isabella danced gracefully, smiling and caught up in her daydream. Elsbeth and Reginald exchanged awkward glances while Margret glared. Isabella stopped dancing and opened her eyes, looking at her stepmother hopefully. Her smile faltered when she saw the look on Margret's face.

MARGRET

I see. Children, what do you think of this? It seems Isabella
wants to go to the ball. Is that right Isabella? You want to go
and dance, maybe even with the prince?

Isabella did not respond, but looked nervous, reading the venom
in Margret's face. Margret lashed out and grabbed Isabella tightly by the arm, pulling her closer to her face and shaking her.

MARGRET

Answer me.

Isabella shakily signed "yes" as tears began forming in her eyes.
Reginald and Elsbeth smirked, watching their mother. Margret
released Isabella's arm and leaned back. She smiled and put her
hands on her hips, turning to give her children a sly look. She
turned back to Isabella.

MARGRET

Do you really think that *you* could go to the ball? I think you
know better than that.

Reginald laughed, then stepped up beside Margret and chimed in.

REGINALD

Come on, *you* at a ball? Actually, that is a great idea. The royal
family might need a new jester!

They all laughed, then Elsbeth joined in and spoke with mock
sincerity.

ELSBETH

Now Reginald, that is ridiculous! Of course Isabella should go to the ball.

Reginald and Margret looked at her in confusion, and Elsbeth continued.

ELSBETH

After all, they might want someone there with Isabella's talents... just in case someone has to stand outside, POINTING the way to the castle!

REGINALD

You know what, that is too true. Hey, with all that signing she does, instead of Isabella, maybe we ought to call her Signerella!

He and Elsbeth burst into laughter and Margret smiled. Isabella turned her head away from them in shame as tears began to roll down her face.

MARGRET

Alright, that is enough fun for now. This girl is beneath us, and teasing her at this point is useless. Let us leave... *Signerella*... to her chores and dreams.

Margret, Elsbeth, and Reginald looked at Isabella and walked away laughing, leaving her standing alone in the middle of the room, crying quietly by herself.

Scene Five

Days passed, and the people in town busied themselves with preparation for the ball. The morning of the grand event finally arrived, and royal announcers were sent throughout the kingdom, riding through towns and declaring the day.

ROYAL ANNOUNCER

Oyez, oyez! The royal ball will commence this evening at 1900 sharp! In honor of the event, His Royal Highness King Philippe Rafael Misael Escorial has declared this day a national holiday! All businesses and shops are to be closed as we prepare for the celebration! His Royal Highness King Philippe, Her Majesty Queen Marisol, and His Royal Highness Prince Misael eagerly await your arrival this evening!

The people's excitement only grew with this announcement, and they continued their preparations for the evening to come.

Meanwhile, back at home in Liata, Isabella went on with her chores as usual. She went out the back door of the house to the small barn area, where the animals waited to be fed. Isabella sat down her bucket of feed and looked kindly at the animals, signing to them.

ISABELLA

Alright animal friends, baby chicks, goat... eat satisfied.

Isabella smiled and began tossing feed to the baby chicks. She watched them eat, signing to them once again.

ISABELLA

Small, cute! Wish you stay small.

She walked over to the goat's pen next and opened the gate to feed him. The goat wandered up to her and nudged her hands with his head, looking for his food. Isabella laughed and began feeding the goat, who ate greedily. Isabella shook her head and signed to the goat as he ate.

ISABELLA

Goat, amazing, eat eat eat! You happy I love you, you not on diet.

After she finished with the goat and other animals, Isabella turned to head inside. Before going back in the house, she took a moment to breathe deep and look up to the sky. Far above, she saw Beto the eagle soaring. Even though she knew he couldn't see her, Isabella sat down her bucket and signed to the bird wistfully.

ISABELLA

B-e-t-o, good morning, you fly! I jealous why? I want free. Fly like you... same hope future me.

Isabella sighed deeply as Beto flew out of sight. She picked up the bucket and walked back into the house. Tiredly, Isabella picked up the broom in the corner or the room and began sweeping the floor. After a short time, Isabella stopped cleaning and put down the broom. She wiped her hands on her skirt and looked around the room, feeling more exhausted, depressed, and alone than ever. On the verge of tears, she turned and ran upstairs to her attic bedroom. Isabella burst into her room and dropped to her knees in front of the small chest where she kept all of her most valued possessions. From it, she pulled out an old, leather-bound book - her mother's Bible. Isabella opened to the back of the Bible and took out a small, worn envelope. She hugged the envelope to her chest, then went and sat on her bed. Isabella gently opened the envelope and took out a letter, and even though she knew the words by heart, she opened the letter and read it carefully:

Dear Isabella,

We want to prepare you, because there will be hard times in this life. People will try to tell you to quit because you are different and sometimes you may want to, but you will be strong and go on. There are those who will expect very little from you, but you will prove them wrong. You are clever and kind, gifted and beautiful. Do not allow anyone to make you doubt that.

Always remember... you are covered by love. No matter where you are, no matter where we are. Our love always covers you.
Love always,
Mama and Papa

Tears rolled down Isabella's face as she read her parents' letter over and over again. She inhaled deeply and sat the letter down, wiping the tears from her face as she stood. Isabella looked out her window and signed sincerely.

ISABELLA
I promise Mama, Papa. Future, I make you proud.

Scene Six

Later that evening, the people of Liata began to leave for the ball. They were dressed in their finest clothes, and the scent of excessive perfumes and colognes hung heavy in the air. At home, Isabella went about her chores as usual when Margret, Elsbeth, and Reginald came downstairs all dressed and ready for the ball. Isabella looked up from her cleaning as they entered the room, then stood and brushed herself off as they approached her with pretentious smiles.

MARGRET
Well *Signerella*, how do we look?

ELSBETH
Please, I already know how fabulous we look. Anyway, we look better than she ever will, that is for sure.

Elsbeth laughed and flipped her hair over one shoulder, then sashayed across the room, giving a little spin to show off her finery. Margret smiled haughtily and turned to Isabella.

MARGRET

Don't you wish you could be beautiful like her, Signerella?

REGINALD

Yes, instead of what you are: a dusty, awful outcast.

Isabella looked hurt momentarily, but sighed deeply and gave a small smile to her stepfamily. She signed to Margret.

ISABELLA

Have fun.

Margret narrowed her eyes suspiciously at Isabella's well wishes. Reginald and Elsbeth exchanged confused glances as Margret stepped closer and spoke directly into Isabella's face.

MARGRET

I don't know why you are pretending to be so understanding and nice, Signerella, but let me be clear-- Your father loved you, and I have tried to treat you fairly for his sake. But he is long gone, and it is past time I tell you the truth. I know you can read my lips, so read this.

Isabella looked shocked and started to step back in fear, but Margret only stepped closer. Even Reginald and Elsbeth looked surprised, but stayed silent, watching everything unfold.

MARGRET

You are no daughter of mine! I consider you nothing but a servant here, an ignorant fool! And that is what you will always be.

Isabella's eyes widened further. She continued to back away, but tripped on a dustpan and fell backwards to the floor. She scrambled to sit up and looked at Margret helplessly. Margret glared down at her with disdain.

MARGRET

Look at you, Signerella. You are pathetic, and you can certainly amount to nothing more than exactly what you are: a weak, helpless servant.

Margret leaned back and stared coldly at Isabella.

MARGRET

Now. If you'll excuse us, we have a ball to attend. Reginald, Elsbeth, let's go! The carriage is waiting.

With one final glare, Margret turned and bounded out of the room. Elsbeth and Reginald followed after her, not even looking in Isabella's direction. The door slammed behind them, and Isabella sat alone on the floor and buried her head in her hands miserably.

Scene Seven

Isabella continued to sit alone in the middle of the floor, feeling more hopeless and alone than ever. She thought to herself.

ISABELLA
All I want is an opportunity. I promised I would make my parents proud, but I am stuck.

With that, she sobbed harder. Suddenly, smoke began to fill the air. Isabella looked around concerned, trying to see if a fire had started somewhere in the room. As she stood and tried to wave the smoke away, a woman appeared in the room right in front of her. To Isabella's shock, the smoke disappeared just as suddenly as it had come. As she took in the woman who now stood before her, Isabella noticed that she looked regal in a royal purple dress and lilac fur coat. On her head, she wore a silver and diamond-encrusted tiara, and she smiled at Isabella with genuine kindness. Isabella finally managed to shake off the shock, and she approached the woman hesitantly. The mysterious woman signed to Isabella.

THE FAIRY GODMOTHER
Hello! I think you need help.

ISABELLA (SIGNING CONFUSEDLY)
Hello... you sign, amazing! But, you who? Two of us meet
before? Help me remember.

THE FAIRY GODMOTHER
If you want know, I tell you.

The woman pulled up a chair from the dining room and sat down
gracefully with a relieved sigh.

THE FAIRY GODMOTHER
All day I stand! Now I feel better. Now I tell you, I your fairy
godmother.

Isabella tilted her head confusedly, scrutinizing the woman
claiming to be her fairy godmother.

ISABELLA
Fairy godmother? Imagine! Guess anything happen.

THE FAIRY GODMOTHER
Very true! You must believe impossible. I-help-you believe.

ISABELLA
Really? Thank you. Don't need help.

THE FAIRY GODMOTHER

You, me believe same. But trust me, things impossible happen end. You believe!

ISABELLA

Sorry, have no idea what you mean. You know, tell me please.

THE FAIRY GODMOTHER

I explain. I know b-a-l-l happen now, right?

Isabella nodded and signed yes, still not following where her fairy godmother was going.

THE FAIRY GODMOTHER

I feel something missing for party. You notice anything missing?

Isabella thinks about it, then shakes her head. The fairy god-mother smiles kindly at Isabella.

THE FAIRY GODMOTHER

You not there. I-help-you arrive there! Follow me please.

The fairy godmother stood and put one arm around Isabella's shoulders, then walked with her out the back door of the house to the barn.

THE FAIRY GODMOTHER
Let's see here...

She looked around, then walked over to the goat's pen. She knelt down delicately and rubbed his head. The fairy godmother signs to the goat and to Isabella.

THE FAIRY GODMOTHER
Hello, goat cute and strong. His name what is?

ISABELLA
No name, call it greedy boy.

The fairy godmother turned back to the goat and signed to him.

THE FAIRY GODMOTHER
Okay, your name greedy boy. Greedy boy, you like become horse now?

The Fairy Godmother smiled and gave the goat one last pat on the head, then stood and turned back to Isabella. Isabella looked confused and signed to her Godmother, asking her what she had just said to the goat. The Fairy Godmother smiled patiently and signed back to her.

THE FAIRY GODMOTHER
I-ask-him want become horse tonight?

ISABELLA
You ask it what? Goat not horse, how happen? Goat, horse? Can't happen.

THE FAIRY GODMOTHER
You wrong. I show proof will. Wait here, bring baby chickens
two, need them.

With that, the Fairy Godmother turned and walked back into
the house. Isabella watched, and though she was still unsure of
what was happening, she walked over to the small coop where the
chickens lived and gently gathered two baby chicks. She waited,
and after a moment, her Godmother came back out of the house
carrying a simple golden apple. The Fairy Godmother came and
stood in front of Isabella, tucking the apple into a pocket on her
dress. She signed to Isabella.

THE FAIRY GODMOTHER
You go party without horse c-a-r-r-i-a-g-e can't, right?

Isabella nodded slowly, wondering nervously if perhaps it was a bad
idea for her to be talking with this strange woman who spoke in rid-
dles. The Fairy Godmother noticed Isabella's uncertainty and gave
a mischievous smile as she pulled the apple back out of her pocket.

THE FAIRY GODMOTHER
Now. Apple delicious there. I take from your kitchen. Everyone
know impossible fruit change c-a-r-r-i-a-g-e, right?

ISABELLA
Right, impossible.

THE FAIRY GODMOTHER
Wrong! Watch.

The Fairy Godmother turned away from Isabella and sat the apple on the ground in front of her. She began to create with her hands, pointing to the apple and signing in the air in front of her:

THE FAIRY GODMOTHER

Apple - huge - there - color - light yellow - gold s-t-e-m - white wheels - with green leaves - windows - circle shape - small door with step.

Isabella watched in amazement as the apple began to change before her very eyes, becoming everything that her Fairy Godmother signed. The Fairy Godmother finished, and with one last flash from her hands, the carriage was complete! Isabella ran up, getting a closer look at the Fairy Godmother's creation. The large, cream-colored carriage looked like something out of a dream. It was apple shaped, but looked elegant with a small gold stem on top of the roof. The spokes of the white wheels were engraved with green leaves that met in the middle of the wheel. On each side of the carriage, there were circular windows lined with gold. To finish it all off, the carriage had one small, golden door and step with a delicate leaf pattern engraved in it. Isabella had never seen anything so beautiful, and she clapped her hands delightedly. The Fairy Godmother watched her with a satisfied, proud look. Isabella turned and signed to her Godmother excitedly.

ISABELLA

Beautiful! Never see before. Thank you!

THE FAIRY GODMOTHER

Fine, dear. Too much gold? You like? Good. Now. Greedy boy, where?

The Fairy Godmother looked around for the goat, who had wandered out of his pen to eat in a small patch of grass not far from where she and Isabella were standing. She marched over to him, and Isabella followed excitedly.

THE FAIRY GODMOTHER

Aha! Goat there, perfect. Can goat change horse? Watch.

The goat looked up at the Fairy Godmother, and just as she had done before, she began creating with her hands. She pointed at the greedy goat and signed her creation.

THE FAIRY GODMOTHER

Goat-change-horse!

The Fairy Godmother gave one last gesture to the goat, signing the letter "h", and suddenly, he was surrounded by a gray smoke. Within a matter of seconds, the smoke disappeared and a beautiful horse stood in the goat's place! The horse was white and looked regal with its light yellow harness, black blinders, and big yellow feather rising from its bridle. Isabella was stunned, and she walked up to the horse, gently petting his nose and feeling his soft mane. She looked back at her Godmother in disbelief.

THE FAIRY GODMOTHER
You still believe things impossible?

ISABELLA
Doubt you, I sorry. He beautiful!

The Fairy Godmother kindly waved away Isabella's apology, already on to the next step in her creation. Looking towards the two baby chicks that were pecking around where Isabella had left them, she signed.

THE FAIRY GODMOTHER
You move there I-s-a-b-e-l-l-a. Next, coachman, footman I need. Baby chicken two, come here please. Wonderful!

Going closer to the two baby chicks, The Fairy Godmother began the magic to turn them into a footman and coachman. Once again, she pointed at the animals and signed her creation into existence.

THE FAIRY GODMOTHER
Baby - chicken - change - adult - men.

Just like before, a cloud of smoke covered the animals, and just as suddenly, two men stood before Isabella and the Fairy Godmother. They stood at attention in front of the carriage, and Isabella smiled, waving her hands to her Godmother in applause.

ISABELLA
Wow! Look like soldiers!

THE FAIRY GODMOTHER
Magic fascinating, right? Now, magic work done! Come hurry,
must ready for b-a-l-l.

The Fairy Godmother briskly ushered Isabella up to the carriage. Isabella looked down at her shabby clothes with some concern, and stopped before they reached the carriage. The Fairy Godmother stopped and looked at her with concern.

THE FAIRY GODMOTHER
What wrong dear?

ISABELLA
Not ready, look at me. Clothes, hair. You go ball look same as
me?

Understanding rushed across the Fairy Godmother's face, and she chuckled and nodded.

THE FAIRY GODMOTHER
You right. You need clothes change, hair fix. Stay, not move,
need finish magic work on you.

Isabella looked relieved and excited. She closed her eyes as her Godmother began her magic. The Fairy Godmother pointed at Isabella and began creating her masterpiece with sign language.

THE FAIRY GODMOTHER
Orange - U neck - dress - orange - small - coat - short - sleeves
- with - orange - fur - gloves - orange - fancy - shoes - h-e-e-l-s

- curly - hair - silk - head band - with - small - d-i-a-m-o-n-d-s - small earrings.

With one final cloud of smoke, Isabella's transformation was complete! She looked down at herself, amazed and impressed by the wonderful work the Fairy Godmother had done. She had dressed her in a long, orange gown made of silk. It had a sheer overcoat that sparkled and shimmered as it caught the light. Beneath the overcoat, a fitted bodice accentuated Isabella's curves perfectly. Where her hair had been messily tied up in an old scarf, it was now curled and pulled back gently in a headband of a slightly darker orange, studded with tiny gems. On her feet were the most beautiful shoes that Isabella had ever seen: deep orange heels that somehow perfectly accentuated the undertones of her dress. To complete the whole look, the Fairy Godmother put on Isabella's hands light orange gloves of the finest satin. The Fairy Godmother had given Isabella a look that matched her personality completely: bright and beautiful. With tears of gratitude forming in her eye, Isabella looked up at her Godmother.

ISABELLA

Godmother, thank you, thank you! This amazing, beautiful. Look like princess!

The Fairy Godmother smiled with pleasure and satisfaction.

THE FAIRY GODMOTHER

Yes, you beautiful. You believe now, understand impossible possible?

ISABELLA

Yes! Now understand, thank you Godmother.

Isabella rushed up to the Fairy Godmother and hugged her tightly. The Fairy Godmother hugged her back, then stepped back and held her by the shoulders gently but firmly.

THE FAIRY GODMOTHER

Now! Go b-a-l-l. Have great time, not nervous. This your chance, you can... I believe you. One rule important: Must leave b-a-l-l when time midnight. All magic work gone will. You see lightning flash, see clock, you know time leave.

Isabella nodded, taking note of her Godmother's rule. They walked up to the carriage together, and the footman helped Isabella up the step and into the carriage, she looked out at her Godmother, nervous and excited.

THE FAIRY GODMOTHER

Remember, twelve midnight, leave! Have fun dear!

Isabella signed thank you one last time, and the carriage began to roll away. She waved out the window to the Fairy Godmother as the carriage drove away until she was no more than a speck in the distance behind her. Isabella sat back in the carriage and waited in nervous anticipation as she made her way to the castle.

Scene Eight

Meanwhile, people from all over the kingdom arrived at the ball. Everyone wore their finest clothes, and excitement was in the air. It was a lively celebration, and the people sipped fine drinks, talked, and mingled before the royal family made their grand entrance. After a short time, a royal announcer came to the top of a staircase leading into the ballroom to announce the arrival of the king, queen, and prince.

ROYAL ANNOUNCER

Atención! The Royal family! His Royal Highness King Philippe, Her Majesty Queen Marisol, and His Royal Highness Prince Misael!

All of the guests stood at attention, silent as the king, queen, and prince entered the room. King Philippe held his wife's hand, and they looked out at the crowd kindly. Prince Misael stood just behind them with a distant smile on his face. Before going to their thrones, the family addressed the people. King Philippe made a speech of welcome.

PHILIPPE

Buenas noches y bienvenidos a todos! On behalf of myself and my queen, welcome to Castillo del Escorial! We are so pleased that you have joined us for this wonderful occasion. We urge you to enjoy yourselves this evening - *come, baila y se feliz*! Though my queen and I dance but very rarely, as we are not as young and spry as we once were (everyone laughed), I am sure our son will be a more than willing and able dance partner for anyone interested. But enough talking - let the festivities begin! Musicians!

As the music began, the king and queen made their way to their thrones and sat to watch the people dancing. The queen looked pointedly at Misael, giving an encouraging nod towards the dance floor. Misael looked uncomfortable, but walked out to the floor in pursuit of a partner. One by one, young women began lining up for their turn to dance with the prince. Misael tried to hide his dread and put on a polite face, taking a turn around the floor with each woman. The king and queen watched with interest from a distance, commenting on each woman and laughing at their son's reactions. The first woman that Misael danced with was a beautiful young woman: well dressed, polite, and elegant. She danced well with the prince, but it was apparent from Misael's expression that the smell of her perfume was entirely too strong. He tried to smile through the dance and be polite, but the king and queen cringed as they saw him barely contain sneeze after sneeze. He attempted to hold the woman farther away from him, but she leaned in closer to speak flirtatiously with him.

DANCE PARTNER #1
May I say, you look absolutely dashing tonight your Highness.

MISAEL
You are too kind.

DANCE PARTNER #1
And I hope this is not too forward of me, Highness, but I am so enjoying this dance.

Misael gave a strained smile and twirled the woman once, then bowed. He thanked her for the dance and waited for her to curtsy and walk away before exhaling deeply. After taking a short moment to catch his breath, Misael bowed to his next partner, who looked as though she might burst into tears. The king and queen looked on with concern.

MARISOL
Good Lord, that poor girl looks positively scared to death!

PHILIPPE
Indeed. I fear she might, cry, be sick, or some combination of both.

MARISOL
For Misa's sake and her own, let us hope neither.

Misael held out his hand to begin dancing, but the woman looked at him with panic, unable to move. Misael shot his parents a confused look, but they merely shrugged and tried to send him encouraging smiles. The prince smiled at the woman and offered his hand again, asking if she would like to dance. The woman put a hand to her stomach, shook her head, and ran away in sheer panic. The prince watched her leave with surprise as the women waiting to dance with him giggled.

MISAEL
Well, she must have been quite nervous.

Misael shook his head and moved on, dancing with the next woman in line. Outside, Isabella's carriage came to a stop, the footman opened the door and helped Isabella to the ground carefully. She looked up at the castle, intimidated by its size and grandeur. The footman placed a hand on her shoulder and looked at Isabella with concern. She shook off her nerves and gave him a reassuring smile, signing to him.

ISABELLA
Thank you.

FOOTMAN
Have fun. Remember 12 midnight leave.

ISABELLA
Yes. Thank you.

Isabella nervously made her way up the steps to the castle. She took a deep breath, then entered confidently, making her way to the ballroom, where the prince was dancing with one partner after another. Misael bowed to a woman, then took a break from dancing to have a drink. As he did, Reginald walked up to him, cup in hand, and struck up a conversation.

REGINALD

Prince Misael, such a pleasure to meet you! I don't know about you, but I am just exhausted from all of this dancing. So many women, so little time, am I right?

Misael looked surprised at Reginald's spontaneous and overly casual address, but smiled and nodded in an attempt to be polite. Reginald continued blathering on.

REGINALD

I can't imagine what it's like being the prince and all. I mean, I have my fair share of eligible and interested women, but they must all positively throw themselves at you! Now that is my kind of trouble.

As Reginald nudged the Prince and smiled lasciviously, Misael looked around uncomfortably, hoping for an excuse to walk away.

MISAEL

Indeed. Well if you will excuse me, it looks like my next partner is waiting for me.

Misael started to walk away. Undeterred, Reginald followed him across the ballroom, speaking loudly.

REGINALD

Yes, I am here from Liata with my mother and sister, Elsbeth. And I have to tell you, Elsbeth has been the talk of the ball! So many men seem impressed by her beauty, grace, and charm. I suppose it's in our blood. All of that, plus our family's immense wealth and connections throughout the kingdom, make her the most eligible woman in this room. Why, whoever has the chance to marry her would be rather lucky indeed.

Misael and Reginald reached the dance floor and approached the prince's next partner, who happened to be Elsbeth. Reginald bowed to the prince.

REGINALD

Well Prince Misael, it has been so nice speaking with you! Enjoy this dance.

As Reginald straightened, he winked at his sister, then turned and walked away. Misael rolled his eyes subtly as he bowed to Elsbeth politely, took her hand and began to waltz. Elsbeth smiled prettily, but struggled to keep up with the steps of the dance. Misael maintained his smile, masking his discomfort with her bad dancing.

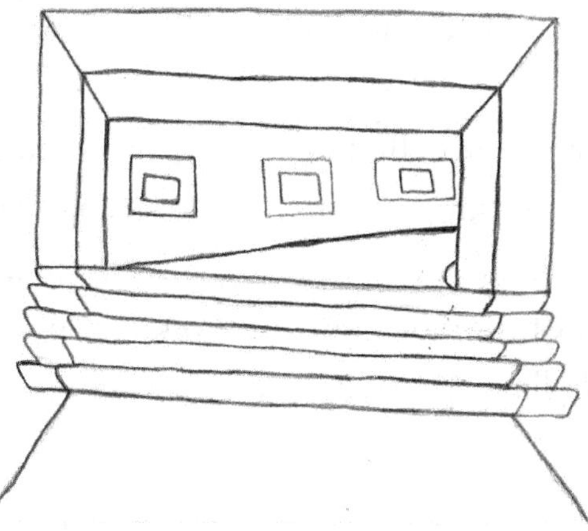

MISAEL

So, where did you learn to dance Señorita?

ELSBETH

Thank you for asking, your highness. Actually, my mother has
been teaching me the steps. I have been improving!

Elsbeth forced a laugh, and Misael tried to laugh along with her,
but grimaced instead as Elsbeth stepped on his toes for what felt
like the hundredth time. At that moment, Isabella found her way
into the ballroom. She stopped at the top of the stairs and looked
around the room, uncertain of where to go or what to do. As he
danced, Misael looked up and saw Isabella standing at the edge of
the ball. He was instantly intrigued by her, and stopped dancing
abruptly.

MISAEL

We have a guest who appears to be lost.

Misael, forgetting about Elsbeth completely, began walking towards Isabella. As he approached, he smiled and spoke.

MISAEL

Good evening, welcome to our ball.

Despite her nerves, Isabella began reading the prince's lips. She
smiled politely and curtsied, but said nothing. Misael was a bit
confused at her silence, not knowing what to make of the lovely
woman in front of him, but wanting to know more. He held out
his hand to Isabella in an invitation.

MISAEL

Would you... care to dance with me?

Isabella smiled bashfully and nodded, but still said nothing. She took the prince's hand, and he led her to the middle of the floor. The king and queen, who had all but given up on their son meeting anyone at the ball, sat up with interest.

PHILIPPE

Did you see that? He just walked right up to her.

MARISOL

Si. Ella es muy hermosa, no?

PHILLIPE

Indeed. Perhaps this will be the something "different" that Misa has been looking for. Let us see...

As the king and queen watched interestedly, Misael walked with Isabella to the center of the ballroom, then looked at her.

MISAEL

Do you know the waltz?

As he spoke, Misael noticed how Isabella watched his face, reading his lips. She did not speak, but nodded her head in answer to his question. Suddenly, realization dawned on him.

MISAEL

Wait, you are not just a quiet type, are you? Is it possible...

The prince signed to Isabella, asking if she was deaf and knew sign language. When she saw Misael sign, Isabella's face lit up in surprise and excitement, and she began signing eagerly.

ISABELLA

Yes, I deaf! You sign? How?

MISAEL

Me HH left ear can't hear. Right ear can hear.

ISABELLA

Oh! You, me, same language.

MISAEL

Yes. My name M-i-s-a-e-l, your name what?

ISABELLA

My name I-s-a-b-e-l-l-a. Nice meet you.

Isabella smiled at the prince, excited to be able to communicate with him. The prince smiled back, and they began dancing the waltz. The crowd of people all looked stunned to see the prince communicating with this mysterious girl using his hands, as they had no idea that he even used Sign Language. They began talking and whispering amongst themselves as everything unfolded. Recognizing the deaf girl to be Isabella, Margret was absolutely shocked and furious. Isabella saw her in the crowd out of the corner of her eye, but ignored her vicious glare and focused on Misael. As they danced, the king and queen looked surprised and pleased at how taken Misael seemed to be with Isabella.

MARISOL

Do you see that *mi amor*? Misael actually looks... happy.

PHILIPPE

He does! You know my dear, I suddenly feel like dancing! Shall
we take to the floor?

Marisol and Philippe smiled slyly at each other, then stood and
walked to the floor. They began dancing, making their way over
to where Misael and Isabella were dancing. As they approached,
the king spoke to his son.

PHILIPPE

Misa! I see you have made a new acquaintance. Perhaps you
should introduce us?

Misael and Isabella paused their dancing as he introduced her to
his parents. Misael spoke and signed so that both Isabella and his
parents could understand him.

MISAEL

Papa, Mama, this is Isabella. Isabella, these are my parents, King
Philippe and Queen Marisol.

Isabella curtsied deeply. When she rose, the king and queen
smiled at her kindly. The queen spoke to her pleasantly.

MARISOL

Welcome Isabella. Might I say, you are a lovely young lady.

Isabella smiled back, then signed to the queen with Misael translating for her.

ISABELLA

Thank you queen, same.

MISAEL

She said thank you, and you are also beautiful.

MARISOL

Ah, you are too kind.

PHILIPPE

Well! We won't keep you young people from enjoying the dance. Isabella, it is a pleasure to meet you. We hope to see you again.

Isabella blushed and smiled, then curtsied once more to the king and queen. The king and queen smiled back at her and Misael, as they resumed their waltz. Misael looked back at Isabella with a gentle look, already falling in love with her. He signed to her, asking if they could continue dancing.

MISAEL

You me dance can?

Isabella smiled dreamily and signed yes. She took the prince's hand, and they began dancing again, gazing into each other's eyes. The other people danced as well, watching Misael and the girl curiously. They continued dancing, oblivious to the eyes of the many onlookers, and made their way out towards the balcony of the ballroom. Once outside, Misael and Isabella stopped dancing after a time and stood, enjoying the beauty of the outdoors and the cool night air. Isabella walked to the railing and leaned over, taking in deep breaths and looking out at the night sky. Misael watched her, and after a moment, walked over and tapped her on the shoulder and signed to her.

MISAEL

You enjoy view?

ISABELLA

Yes, love outside.

MISAEL

I see that before, many times

ISABELLA

Meaning?

MISAEL

I grow-up see beautiful nature. I wish someone with me
appreciate nature

ISABELLA

You not meet someone yet? Surprising! You kind, smart...
handsome.

Isabella smiled bashfully. Misael smiled back, and she continued signing.

ISABELLA

You mean lot me. Two-of-us connect, same understand. We live different world, me deaf, you hard-hearing. Two-of-us should equal. You prince, beautiful kingdom you have. People think you satisfied, happy. But you want someone not think about your title or kingdom but see your inside, love real you. Before parents die, they warn me, life make you feel less important. But I know me, strong. If you not prince, not have wealth, you like me - ordinary person. I not see you that way, like prince. I see you person like me: strong, with heart. I care real you.

Misael watched Isabella sign, struck by how beautiful she looked with the stars shining behind her and the light from the party behind them lighting up her face. He knew that she understood just how he felt, and loved her even more because she truly connected with him as more than just the prince. He had never met anybody who understood him so well, and knew even from their short time together that he wanted to be with Isabella forever. As she finished signing, he responded to her passionately.

MISAEL

You real amazing, wonderful. You understand.

Misael and Isabella smiled and looked into each other's eyes. Misael leaned forward hesitantly, and he and Isabella shared a kiss. As they broke apart, Misael held Isabella close to him for a moment. She closed her eyes, leaning into his embrace. After some time, Misael let go of Isabella and began signing to her.

MISAEL

I-s-a-b-e-l-l-a, we have something no one have. Me happy you appreciate. I love you. How you feel if I-ask-you...

Before Misael could finish signing, a sudden bolt of lightning lit up the sky. Isabella looked around in surprise and saw in the distance the clock tower of the castle, just beginning to ring midnight. She remembered her Godmother's warning, and as thunder began to roll, she signed quickly to Misael and began to run away.

ISABELLA

Oh! Time, I leave now! Good bye!

MISAEL

Wait, please wait!

Misael tried to get Isabella's attention waving his hands frantically as she ran away from him, but she kept going. Isabella tore back through the ballroom, and the crowd looked on in shock as the prince ran after her. By the sixth ring of the clock bell, Isabella was making her way hurriedly down the front steps of the castle. She tried to take her gloves off as she ran, and managed to get one off, but dropped it on the steps. As she

made it outside, she saw her carriage, with the footman waving for her to hurry inside. Isabella made it into the carriage, and they sped off into the night. By the time Misael made it outside, Isabella's carriage was riding off into the distance. He watched it, and stood for a moment in complete despair. Just as he was about to turn and go back inside, Misael noticed Isabella's glove lying at the foot of the stairs. He walked down and picked it up, holding to his heart and looking sadly out into the distance.

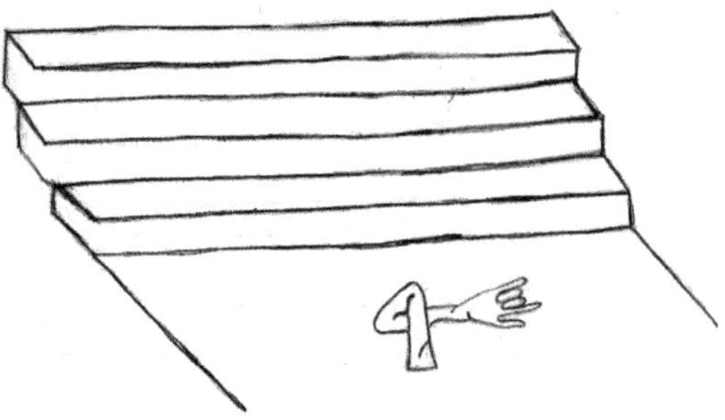

Later that evening, Isabella finally made it home. Her horse, coachman, and footman had turned back into themselves, and her carriage turned back into an apple, which the greedy goat proceeded to eat. Isabella walked back to the barn and put the animals back where they belonged, thanking them for their help even though she knew they didn't really understand her. She went back into the house and up to her attic bedroom, grateful that her stepfamily wasn't back yet and she had some time alone to think about all that had happened that night. She smiled dreamily, remembering how it felt to be in Misael's arms. Suddenly, Isabella felt something in her pocket. She reached down and pulled it out, surprised to see one of her orange silk gloves. She smiled gratefully, holding the glove to her heart. Isabella put the glove back in her pocket and signed.

ISABELLA
Thank you, thank you Godmother. Me never forget this night. Thank you much.

Scene Nine

Isabella woke early the next morning, refreshed from a night of dreams filled with Misael. She reached into her right pocket and pulled out her orange glove, smiling as the memories all rushed back to her. Isabella got out of bed and pretended she was dancing with Misael once again, waltzing around the room with a dreamy smile on her face. She waltzed over to the window and looked out, imagining that she could see the castle in the distance. As she looked out the window, Isabella saw Gilberto the golden eagle perched on a tree. It looked to her as though Beto was looking right at her, and Isabella gave a friendly smile and signed to him.

ISABELLA
B-e-t-o! Morning beautiful, correct? Beautiful day, you know.
Flying, you can see me, castle... anything you want see.

Isabella smiled and walked away from the window. She closed her eyes once again, imagining herself dancing in Misael's arms once more. As she waltzed around the small room with her eyes closed, the door slammed open, and Margret stormed in furiously. Isabella obliviously kept dancing until Margret stalked up and tapped her shoulder, hard. Isabella's eyes flew open and she whirled around, startled, to see Margret glaring at her. Margret began to speak, spitting words in Isabella's face.

MARGRET

You little wench... how dare you?! You know that I saw you at that ball last night, *Signerella*, correct? Yes or no!

Isabella looked afraid for a moment, but took a deep breath and stood up straight. She looked directly into Margret's face and nodded once, signing yes. Margret's eyes flashed dangerously, then she became completely composed. She stared at Isabella for a long moment, then spoke.

MARGRET

That's what I thought. I don't know how you managed to get to the ball, dressed like... that, but I won't tolerate such deception from a servant under my roof.

Before Isabella knew what was happening, Margret lashed out and grabbed her tightly by the arm, dragging her out of the room and down the stairs. She kept going, mercilessly dragging Isabella all the way to the cold, dark basement of the house. She threw Isabella inside, then turned to speak coldly, with the light behind her wicked face.

MARGRET

You need to learn, Signerella. You are a servant in this house - you have no privileges and no rights. You will stay down here as punishment until further notice.

With that, Margret slammed the door shut and locked it, sending the room into darkness. Isabella looked around, trying to find some way out, but saw only a small window at the top of the far wall. She tried to look out and see if there was anybody who could help her, but not a single person passed by. Isabella sat back and took a frustrated breath, then sank to her knees and prayed for some miracle to make it out.

Back at the castle, Misael was inconsolable about the loss of Isabella. The king and queen sat with him, trying to help him feel better, but were having very little success.

MARISOL

Try to cheer up Misa, it is not all bad. I could tell that she was just as smitten with you as you were with her; she *must* have had a perfectly good reason for running away so suddenly!

Misael said nothing, but only looked miserably down at Isabella's glove, which he still held in his hand.

PHILIPPE

Son, *tu madre tiene razón*. It wasn't your fault, we are sure of it! There must be something we can do. Surely there is a way to find her.

MISAEL

No, there is nothing to be done! I only know her first name. I don't know her surname, what town she comes from... nothing. I cannot believe it. I finally find the person I want to spend the rest of my life with, and I have lost her just as suddenly.

As the king watched Misael looking at Isabella's glove, he was struck with a brilliant idea.

PHILIPPE
¡Lo *sé!* I know exactly what to do!

Misael and Marisol looked up at him in surprise, eagerly waiting to hear Philippe's plan.

PHILIPPE
Misael, if you believe you love this girl as much as you say, then we must find her. Let us search the kingdom. We will send out the chamberlains, and tell them to go to every house with a daughter, searching for a deaf girl who uses Sign Language. If they find her, the final test will be to have her try on this glove that you have to prove that it is really her. What do you think?

MISAEL
Oh Papa, I think that is an excellent idea! Let us begin right away, we haven't a moment to lose. This could take days, but it will work, I know that it will!

Philippe hurriedly called for six chamberlains and instructed them to go out into the kingdom, far and wide, until they found Misael's love. Having their orders, the chamberlains set out that day in search of Isabella. Over the next three days, they went from town to town, having no success. Hearing that the prince was looking for his lost love, women all over the kingdom started preparing for the chamberlain's visit. They would pretend to be deaf, using fake sign language or bits and pieces of signs to fool the chamberlain. They all failed, though, when it came to the glove, which had been designed specifically by the Fairy Godmother's magic to fit only Isabella's hands. On the third day, weary from his travels, a chamberlain finally made it to Liata. Margret, hearing of his arrival, began scheming to make Elsbeth the girl the prince was looking for.

Meanwhile, Isabella was still locked in the basement. She had been alone for three days, with only Elsbeth coming twice a day to bring her water and a small bowl of leftover table scraps. As Isabella sat at the window, she saw the horses of the royal chamberlains drive by on their way to the front of the house. Weak from hunger, she had no time to react before they rode past her window. Still, Isabella sat up in excitement.

ISABELLA
Yes, he still love me! He know me here.

More determined than ever, Isabella thought hard to find some way out of her basement dungeon. Suddenly, she was inspired with an idea as she saw the greedy goat wandering not far away, eating some grass. She pulled the glove out of her pocket, held it to her heart, and then started waving it out the window, hoping that the goat would see it and be drawn over by the color, thinking it was hay or anything else he might eat.

Back upstairs, Margret called for Elsbeth as the chamberlain arrived at the door.

MARGRET

Elsbeth! Come quickly, girl! Hurry and fix yourself, the
chamberlain is here!

Elsbeth rushed downstairs nervously, with Reginald following
behind her, just as Margret opened the door and welcomed the
chamberlain inside. Since she knew some Sign Language, she
had taught some words to Elsbeth and managed to convince the
chamberlain that she was deaf.

At the same time, Isabella finally managed to get the goat's attention
with her glove. Since Reginald, Elsbeth, and Margret had carelessly
left his pen open for the past few days, the goat easily ambled over
to where Isabella was. As he came close, Isabella quickly pulled the
glove inside and waited, knowing that the curious and greedy goat
would butt the window in to get to the food he thought was inside.
She waited as he did just that, slamming the glass out of the window
with one solid ram of his horns. Relieved, Isabella patted the goat on
the nose as he looked around for some food.

ISABELLA

Good boy.

Seeing that there was nothing to eat, the goat ambled away casu-
ally. Isabella used all of her strength to pull herself up and out of
the now fully open window.

Meanwhile, Margret tried to convince the chamberlain to stay, despite the fact that Elsbeth's hand had of course not fit into the glove.

MARGRET

Please, let her try it on one more time! She just needed to
stretch her hands a bit more, but she's definitely ready for the
glove now.

Elsbeth forgot that she was supposed to be pretending to be deaf
and nodded emphatically as she yelled.

ELSBETH

It's true! I'm ready now.

She realized her mistake too late, and the chamberlain sighed
and rolled his eyes impatiently.

CHAMBERLAIN

Señora, you have wasted enough of my time. Your daughter is
most certainly not deaf and the glove will not fit. If you will
excuse me, I will be going now.

The chamberlain opened the door and was just beginning to
walk away when a disheveled Isabella ran up from the back of the
house. The chamberlain was shocked, taking in her dirty and exhausted face, but stopped. Margret, Elsbeth and Reginald came
to the door, hearing the commotion. As she saw Isabella standing
in front of the chamberlain, Margret was enraged. She walked
outside just as Isabella began signing to the chamberlain.

CHAMBERLAIN

What is this? And who are you, *Señorita*?

ISABELLA

Please, my name I-s-a-

Margret interrupted Isabella's signing, standing in front of her and speaking to the chamberlain.

MARGRET

Please sir, just ignore this girl. She is my insolent servant... she is not even supposed to be out here! I apologize for her presence.

The chamberlain looked at Margret with distaste and respectfully moved her aside.

CHAMBERLAIN

All due respect, *Señora*, I think I will see for myself. This girl seems to know Sign Language, and my orders are to give *every* girl in the kingdom a chance. Now, if you will excuse me.

Isabella smiled and signed to the chamberlain once more.

ISABELLA

Put on glove can I?

CHAMBERLAIN

I am not entirely sure of what you are saying, but let's have you try on the glove.

The chamberlain pulled out Isabella's glove, and she beamed. Just as he was about to put it on her hand, Margret, in a rage, ran over and snatched the glove out the chamberlain's hand. She stuffed her hand in it, viciously tearing through the seams and leaving the glove in pieces.

CHAMBERLAIN

Dios mio! Why would you do such a thing? What am I to do now? His Highness will be most displeased with me!

As Margret huffed and the chamberlain looked distraught at the pieces of glove, Isabella reached her hand into her pocket and subtly pulled on the other glove. All of a sudden, she pulled her hand out of her pocket and victoriously waved the glove around for everyone to see.

CHAMBERLAIN

The other glove! Surely this young lady is the one!

He looks at Isabella and speaks excitedly as she reads his lips.

CHAMBERLAIN

I believe His Highness has been looking for you, my dear. Come with me, I shall take you to the castle!

Isabella smiles brightly and leaves with the chamberlain, not looking back at her stepfamily once. Margret started crying angrily and kicking the dirt, and Elsbeth and Reginald watched somberly as Isabella rode off to the castle.

Scene Ten

The next morning, Prince Misael stood at his window as he had for the past four days, anxiously waiting for any word about the search. Down the road, he saw one of the chamberlains arriving on horseback with a young woman. Without hesitation, Misael ran down to the front of the castle and waited as the chamberlain rode up. He dismounted and helped Isabella down from the horse as well.

CHAMBERLAIN
Your highness, I have found her! The girl you were looking for, I am sure of it!

Misael heard the chamberlain, but paid him little attention as he focused on Isabella. She looked away shyly, a bit embarrassed at her disheveled appearance, but Misael didn't care. He stepped up to Isabella boldly and looked into her eyes. They smiled at one another in recognition, and Misael embraced her tightly. They separated, and Misael signed excitedly.

MISAEL

They have found you! I-s-a-b-e-l-l-a, I love you. I want you in kingdom with me please. Marry me?

ISABELLA

Of course! I love you. I want share kingdom with you.

Misael and Isabella kissed and embraced once more as King Misael and Queen Marisol came downstairs, having heard the chamberlain arrive. They stood at the top of the stairs and smiled at Misael and Isabella as they embraced joyously.

Not long after that day, the wedding of Price Misael and Princess Isabella took place in the royal courtyard. It was a grand ceremony, and people came from all over the kingdom to celebrate the wedding of their beloved prince and his lovely new bride. As she celebrated with her love, Isabella saw her Fairy Godmother in the distance, smiling and waving her hands in applause. She smiled gratefully and put her hand over her heart as her Godmother signed.

THE FAIRY GODMOTHER

Impossible, possible!

Isabella beamed and waved as her Godmother disappeared. In the sky above, Beto the golden eagle flew by! She thought to herself.

ISABELLA

My friends are here to celebrate with me! Thank you Fairy Godmother, because of you, I know that I can expect the impossible! Beto, fly free... now I am free too. Mama, Papa, I wish you were here. But now I will make you proud, just like you always believed I would.

Isabella smiled over at Misael, who looked back at her contentedly. They held hands and made their way to their carriage, waiting to take them away. As they entered the carriage, Misael and Isabella looked out at the crowds of people. They waved to the king and queen, who stood arm in arm, smiling from ear to ear as they watched them leave. Misael tapped Isabella on the shoulder and signed as she turned to face him.

MISAEL

Dear I-s-a-b-e-l-l-a. Together, we royalty. Together, we strong. I love you.

ISABELLA

Yes my love. We belong together, forever.

Isabella smiled at Misael, and they kissed as the carriage began to pull away from the castle. When they broke apart, Misael and Isabella turned and waved out the window joyfully as they rode away into the sun.

THE END.

www.ingramcontent.com/pod-product-compliance
Lightning Source LLC
Chambersburg PA
CBHW062347121125
35392CB00053B/2355

9 781649 902832